Fuzzy Wuzzy

by
Norma
Charles

Illustrated
by
Galan
Akin

A Hodgepog Book

All characters in this story are fictitious.

Hodgepog Books acknowledges the ongoing support of the
Canada Council for the Arts.

Editors: Luanne Armstrong and Dorothy Woodend

Cover design and inside layout by Linda Uyehara Hoffman
Set in Greymantle MVB and Bookman in Quark XPress 4.1
Printed at Hignell Book Printing

A Hodgepog Book for Kids

Published in Canada by Hodgepog Books,
3476 Tupper Street
Vancouver, BC
V5Z 3B7
Telephone (604) 874-1167
Email: woodend@telus.net

National Library of Canada Cataloguing in Publication Data

Charles, Norma M.
  Fuzzy wuzzy

  ISBN 0-9730831-2-3

  I. Title.

PS8555.H4224F89   2002   jC813'.54   C2002-910954-X
PZ7.C3783Fu   2002

The Canada Council | Le Conseil des Arts
for the Arts | du Canada

Fuzzy Wuzzy

Table of Contents

Chapter 1	Enemy Number One	1
Chapter 2	Mean Old Miley Strikes Again	9
Chapter 3	An Old Friend	18
Chapter 4	Kate's Secret Magic Spell	21
Chapter 5	Ted's Birthday Party	25
Chapter 6	Entertaining Fierce Four-Year-Olds	34
Chapter 7	Party Rap	42
Chapter 8	A Friend Indeed	48

Chapter 1
Enemy Number One

One summer morning when the sun was shining like a big round lemon drop, Ruby was skipping home from Joe's Bakery. Summer holidays were the best!

She was swinging a bag of fresh Jamaican patties. The delicious spicy aroma made her mouth water.

Suddenly, out from the bushes popped her enemy number one, Mean Old Miley.

Ruby gripped the bag of Jamaican patties tight and tried to escape, but Mean Old Miley held out his stick and wouldn't let her pass. He

was the meanest kid in the whole neighbourhood. Certainly the meanest kid in their grade three class. Probably the meanest kid in the whole school. Maybe even in the whole country!

He pulled down his baseball cap and growled at her. "Ha, ha!" he shouted. "Got you, Fuzzy Wuzzy!"

Ruby tried to push past him but he cartwheeled around her and started his rap. Banging his stick on the sidewalk in front of her to keep time, he shouted:

Fuzz Ball, Fuzz Ball
Comin' from the Mall.
Fuzz Ball, Fuzz Ball,
And that's not all,
Fuzz Ball, Fuzz Ball,
Fat as a wall.
Fuzz Ball, Fuzz Ball!
Yeah! Yeah! Yeah!

He thought he was about the best rapper around. But his teasing raps poked at Ruby until her insides felt as hollow as a big drum.

"Fuzzy, Fuzzy Wuzzy," he taunted, his head bobbing up and down.

Ruby's face flooded with anger. She was

mad. Very, very mad. She clenched her hands into fists and yelled back at him. "Freckle, freckle face! You're a stupid old, dirty old freckle face! So there!"

She turned to get away from him and dash home. But she tripped over a rock and wrenched her ankle.

Down she tumbled, scraping her knee on the gritty sidewalk, and scattering the fresh Jamaican patties into the dust.

"Ha, ha!" shouted Mean old Miley.

Now Fuzzy Wuzzy can't even walk!
Fuzzy Wuzzy can't even talk.
Fuzz Ball's chewin' on a bone.
Fuzz Ball's crawlin' on home! Yeah!

Ruby's eyes stung with tears. She could hardly see the gritty patties as she stuffed them back into the bag. She got up and brushed off her knees. Then she turned her back on Mean old Miley and limped the rest of the way home.

● ● ●

Her mother was putting down the phone when Ruby came in the back door and limped into the kitchen.

"Ruby! What ever happened to you?" she asked.

"I-I just tripped on a rock and fell," mumbled Ruby.

"Oh sweetie. Are you hurt?"

"No. Just a scrape on my knee."

"Let's see." Her mother wiped the dirt off Ruby's knee with the hem of her skirt. "It doesn't look too bad. Not bleeding, at least. But I bet it really hurt."

Ruby nodded and sniffed.

"But look at the patties!" said her mother. "They're all dirty! You must have dropped them. You'll have to go back to Joe's and get more. We couldn't eat these for lunch."

"I don't want to go back to Joe's, Mom," Ruby shook her head. "Do I have to?"

"Are you sure you're all right, my sweet?" Her mother gently patted Ruby's curly hair.

"Sure, I'm all right. But I don't want to go back to Joe's." Ruby sniffed again and wiped her nose on the back of her hand.

She wanted to tell on Miley, but then he would call her Tattle-tale Fuzzy Wuzzy. Or Rat Fink Fuzzy Wuzzy! He was as mean as an old skunk.

Her mother handed her a tissue and she blew her nose.

"I have to finish the Doberman project this morning so I can't go to the bakery myself," she said. "And Ruby, guess who phoned this morning. Kate's mother! She and Kate are in town so I invited them over for lunch today!"

"Kate Sands?" Ruby felt her face brighten.

Her mother nodded. "Yes. We haven't seen them for a long time, have we? Ever since they moved away last year."

"Great! Kate's really fun. Yippee!"

"So you see, we do need those patties. Could you please go now and get some more? Remember how much Kate and her mother love Joe's Jamaican patties. They're the best in the west."

"All right. I guess I'll go. I'll just comb my hair first."

● ● ●

Ruby took a long look at herself in the bathroom mirror. Her round dark eyes stared back at her.

"Miley's right," she told herself wiping away the smudges her tears had left. "This dumb hair is all fuzzy wuzzy. It's so ugly! No wonder he makes fun of it. And that's probably why everyone always stares at me. It's this stupid, ugly, fuzzy wuzzy hair!"

She tugged at her brown curls, wishing she would yank them all right out.

Her dad's bottle of hair cream was on the shelf beside the sink. **End the Frizzies Today**, it declared on the label.

She opened the bottle and poured a big gob onto her hair and rubbed it in. It smelled nice. Like her dad. With a comb, she carefully parted her hair as close to the centre of her head as she could.

Then she pressed down the hateful fuzz flat on both sides of her face, glued it down with more hair cream and pinned it.

She brushed her hair some more and she pinned it down with hairpins. She pinned it and she brushed it and pinned it some more.

After a while, her hair was a smooth sleek cap, all around her head.

"Hey there! No more frizzies. Lookin' good," she said, grinning at herself in the mirror. Her smile pushed her cheeks into dimples. "Now Mean old Miley sure can't call me Fuzzy Wuzzy Fuzz Ball."

"Hurry, Ruby!" called her mother. "It's almost lunch time and I'd like to have lunch ready before our friends arrive."

Ruby was still grinning when she walked into the kitchen with her new sleek hair-do.

"Ruby! What on earth have you done to your hair!"

"It's my new hair-do," said Ruby, holding her head as carefully as a fragile package. "How do you like it?"

"It's certainly very, um, very tidy looking," said her mother, patting the pins gently. "Yes indeed. Very tidy. Now, here's the money for the patties. When you cross the street, mind you don't forget to watch the cars."

"I won't," said Ruby automatically. Her mother always said, "Watch the cars."

Chapter 2
Mean Old Miley Strikes Again

On her way out the back door, Ruby picked up her brother Sam's Seraptor action figure. It was gruesome looking, with long white fangs and a green face. She put it into her shorts pocket. It would keep her company.

She could not believe that she was actually missing her brother. She even missed playing street hockey with him and his buddies. He would be gone for one more week at the summer sports camp.

Joe's Bakery was only across the street and two short blocks away, but she would have to walk right past Mean old Miley's house again. Unless she went the long way. But that would make it 1,2,3,4,5 blocks longer, Ruby counted on her fingers.

No, she decided. It was not worth it.

She started out the usual way. She patted her pocket. She had Sam's Seraptor action figure to guard her against any attackers. Especially the mean, rapping acrobat kind.

Holding her head as level as she could, to

protect her new hair-do, Ruby glanced up the street and down the street. No cars, so she skimmed across. Then, as sophisticated as a high fashion model on TV, she glided up the block and turned the corner.

Quietly, so very quietly, she tiptoed past the bushy hedge that surrounded Miley's house. She held her breath.

Miley was sure to leap out any second. But he would see her with her new smoothed-down, sleek hair-do, so now he couldn't call her anything like Fuzzy Wuzzy Fuzz Ball.

Ruby's feet started to scamper, but she stopped them.

If Miley saw her run past his place, he would think she was scared. Then he would make up another rap about her. He would call her Chicken-livered-Scaredy-Cat- Fuzz-Ball. Or maybe even Fuzzy-Wuzzy-Chicken-Livered-Scaredy-Cat-Fuzz-Ball!

She was about to slink past the very last bush when she saw a branch move. She caught her breath and froze!

"Meow!" It was only a small grey kitten.

Ruby sprinted all the rest of the way to Joe's Bakery.

● ● ●

On her way home, she saw her friend, Allison. She was playing skip with her little brother, Ted on their front sidewalk. They had tied one end of the skipping rope to their porch and Ted was trying to turn the rope over Allison's head but most of the time, it got caught in her blond ponytail.

She always had to look after Ted these days, since they had a new baby sister at their house.

"Hey, Ruby," she called. "Want to come and play skip with us?"

"Can't. I have to hurry home. Mom's waiting for these patties for lunch."

"Ruby! You look so different!" said Allison. "Did your mom brush your hair like that?"

"No." Ruby held her head as still as a cloud so she would not disturb the pins. "I did it all by myself. It's my new hair-do."

"Now you look like a real grown-up lady," said Ted in his deep, serious, little boy voice.

Ruby grinned at the compliment.

"Can't you have just one quick turn of Blue Bells with us, please?" pleaded Allison. "Ted and me, we'll turn the rope for you."

"Well, okay. I guess so," said Ruby. "Just a quick turn."

She set the bag of Jamaican patties down on Allison's front steps and joined them skipping Blue Bells. She jumped into the turning rope.

"Blue bells. Cockle shells..." they sang while Ruby skipped.

One of her curls popped up. Then another. And another! Soon her whole head was a puff of brown curls again.

Her foot tangled in the rope.

"You're out," shouted Allison.

"Ruby! Your new hair-do!" said Ted. "It's all gone!"

Ruby felt her head. "Oh no!" she squealed. All those ugly curls had sprung back up. Every single one. Now she was Fuzzy Wuzzy again.

"My hair!" she cried. "I have to get home."

She dashed down the sidewalk towards her house.

She rounded the corner.

Out from the bushes, like a somersaulting jack-in-the-box, popped up Mean old Miley!

He grabbed a stick and hopped in front of Ruby. He stuck the stick out like a police officer stopping traffic.

No Fuzzy Wuzzy
Allowed past my house.
Not even if she
Crawls like a mouse
A fuzzy wuzzy mouse.

He poked his stick at Ruby.

She shrank back. For a second, she had forgotten about Mean old Miley. She was not expecting him. And here, her sleek new hair-do was gone!

Mean old Miley cartwheeled around her. Then he leapt in front of her again and, hitting the sidewalk with his stick to keep time, he shouted out a rap in her face:

Fuzzy Wuzzy was a bear

But Fuzzy Wuzzy had a lot of hair
And that's not all
Fuzzy Wuzzy was Fuzzy Wuzzy Fuzz Ball!
Fuzz Ball! Fuzz Ball! Fuzz Ball! Yeah!!

He did a quick one-handed cartwheel. He leapt up and was about to start rapping again.

But by this time Ruby was hot with anger. Hot as the most fiercely hot summer day.

She jammed her hand into her pocket and pulled out her brother's Seraptor action figure.

"You leave me alone!" she yelled into Mean

old Miley's face. "You big ugly freckle faced baboon!"

And that's not all,
Fuzz Ball, Fuzz Ball, Fuzz Ball! he taunted.

He pole-vaulted over the fire hydrant and landed directly in front of her again.

She threw Seraptor right, smack, into the middle of his freckled teasing grin.

"Yow!" he yelled. He dropped his stick and grabbed his nose. Blood oozed between his fingers.

He howled like a lost dog. "My nose! You hit my nose! Look, my nose! There's blood on it! It's blee-eeding!"

Ruby's stomach tightened. She spun away and raced across the street. She ran and ran. She did not stop running until she reached her own front door.

"Mom!" she shouted, trying to catch her breath as she stumbled into the house. She caught a glimpse of herself in the mirror in the front hall. Her hair was sticking up all over the place.

"Scissors! Where are those scissors! I'm cutting it all off. This fuzzy wuzzy stupid hair. Every single bit! I hate it! Hate it! So ugly, I can't stand it one more minute!"

She yanked open the drawer in the hall table. Scissors! There they were! She grabbed them. She fumbled to get her fingers into the holes. She would slash off this horrible ugly hair right this second.

"Ruby! Stop!" Her mother caught her arm and took the scissors away. She put them back into the drawer and shut it firmly. She held Ruby's hand and gently tilted her chin to look into her face.

"Now, Ruby. Think! You can't cut off all your hair. How would you look with no hair at all? Surely, that's not what you want."

"But this hair is so ugly! I hate it! Hate it! Everyone always stares at me and teases me. I can't stand it!" wailed Ruby. "Why can't I have nice straight-down hair like you do?"

Her mother stroked her cheek. "But you have beautiful hair, my pet. I don't understand why you don't like it. It's all so soft and fluffy. You take after your dad's side of the family. Everyone on his side has curly hair. Here, now. Wipe your tears." She gave her a couple of tissues.

Just then the front door bell rang.

Ruby gasped. "Oh no! That must be Miley's mother coming to tell Mom about Miley's bleeding nose. Am I ever in for it now! Where can I hide?"

Chapter 3
An Old Friend

But it was not Miley or Miley's mother.

It was Kate and her mother.

"Come in. Come in." Ruby's mother greeted them. "How lovely to see you two again. It's been ages."

Ruby wiped her eyes and stared at Kate. She was a pretty as a spring morning with a short green flowered skirt and matching top. And her hair! A wide beaded hair band held her curly brown hair. Ruby had not seen her for so long that she had forgotten that Kate had curly hair as well. Just like hers!

"Here's a present for you, Ruby," said Kate, handing her a parcel wrapped in blue tissue paper. "I made it myself for you. Go on. Open it."

Ruby tore open the parcel. It was a beaded hair band!

"One just like yours, except blue. My favourite colour. Thanks, Kate! I love it!"

"Here, I'll help you put it on, if you like." Kate tucked Ruby's fluff into the hair band.

"Oh, that's so pretty, Ruby," said her mother. "I love your hair like that." She turned to Kate's mother and said, " We'll have lunch soon. Ruby got some of those delicious spicy Jamaican patties from Joe's Bakery."

"Great," said Kate's mother. "I haven't tasted such good patties since we left town."

"Where did you put the bag of patties, Ruby?" asked her mother.

"Patties? Oh no! I must have left them at Allison's house."

"What! Those patties must be jinxed. First you dropped them on the sidewalk. And now you forgot them. Will you please go and get them right this minute."

"But I can't, Mom. I really can't." Ruby's stomach knotted and her eyes stung with tears again. Mean old Miley was sure to be waiting to pounce on her and beat her up. Especially now that she had given him a bleeding nose.

"Ruby. Allison's house is only a block away. You go there by yourself all the time. What ever is the matter?"

"I could go with you," offered Kate, smiling at Ruby.

Ruby looked at Kate. She was bigger than Mean old Miley. And probably stronger as well. She stood so straight and tall that no one would ever tease her.

"All right," she said. "If you come with me, Kate."

Chapter 4
Kate's Secret Magic Spell

When they were outside, Ruby said to Kate, "Can I ask you something?"

"Sure. Go right ahead."

"Do kids ever tease you about, you know, your curly hair? Like call you Fuzzy Wuzzy or Fuzz Ball, or stuff like that?"

"They used to. Especially one tall skinny girl whose name's Ronny. It's funny, because, after a while, we got to be really good friends. In fact, now she's my best friend in our new neighbourhood."

"How did that happen?"

Kate lowered her voice. She said, "I've discovered a secret weapon against teasers. It's something like putting a magic spell on them."

"Magic? There's really no such thing as magic. Is there?" A shiver worked its way up Ruby's back. A magic spell! She really wanted to believe Kate.

"Maybe it's not exactly magic. But it surely works like magic."

"Okay. How does it work?" Ruby bit her lip

with excitement.

"I'll tell you."

After checking that there wasn't anyone around listening, Kate whispered her secret into Ruby's ear.

Ruby shook her head. "That sounds impossible," she said. "I'll bet it would never work in a million years on that Mean old Miley."

"You don't think so? All I can say is that it worked for me. So why don't you give it a try? What have you got to lose?"

"We have to walk past his place to get the patties anyway," said Ruby. "So we'll probably see him."

"Good."

When they got to Miley's yard, they crept by on tip-toe. The leaves on the bushes shivered in the breeze. But no Miley.

They went to Allison's house and got the bag of patties from the front steps where Ruby had left it. Allison and her little brother weren't there.

On the way home they had to pass Mean old Miley's bushes again. They were almost all the way past when he dropped out of a tree. Right in front of them!

He cartwheeled around them, grabbed his long stick and started his rapping.

Two Fuzzy Wuzzys
Can't go by my house
Not even if they're
Quiet as a mouse
Quiet as a louse
Quiet as a mouse.
Yeah! Yeah! Yeah!

As he rapped, he pranced around them, bobbing his head, his mouth open so wide that

Ruby could have counted his teeth. Not that she wanted to.

She was about to dash back home. But Kate poked her in the ribs.

"Here's your chance," she hissed. "Come on. Do it!"

Ruby stood as tall and straight as a pole. She clenched her fists and took a deep breath. She stared at Mean old Miley, right square in the eye.

He screwed up his ugly freckled nose at her. Then he stuck out his fat tongue. He was all set to start another rap.

Ruby could not stand it. No way could she follow Kate's instructions for the magic spell.

"Come on," she said, grabbing Kate's arm and pulling her away.

● ● ●

"But why didn't you just try it," asked Kate, panting when they reached Ruby's house.

"I couldn't," cried Ruby. "I just couldn't."

"Oh well. Maybe you can try again some other day."

Chapter 5
Ted's Birthday Party

There's nothing more dreary than a dark rainy morning in the middle of your summer holidays, thought Ruby, after breakfast, a few days later.

She stared out her bedroom window at the rain dripping on the leaves and the grass. This day was no good for swimming. No good for bike riding. No good for street hockey. No good for anything at all. She dressed slowly, pulling on her T-shirt and shorts, wondering what to do.

Maybe Allison could think of something. When Ruby thought of Allison's little brother, she grinned. He was such a serious little guy in a cute, funny way.

She tucked her hair into her new hair band and called, "Mom. I'm going over to play with Allison."

"All right, sweetie," said her mother from her study. "See you at lunch time. Mind you watch the cars now."

One good thing about the rain, Ruby thought as she zipped up her raincoat and pulled down her hood. At least Mean old Miley probably wouldn't be around, waiting to pounce on her. She looked both ways and crossed the empty street. When she walked by Miley's place, she held her breath, ready to start running, but there wasn't any sign of him. She sighed with relief when she turned the corner to go to Allison's house.

When Allison opened her front door and saw that it was Ruby, she grabbed her sleeve and pulled her inside. "Oh, Ruby! I'm so glad that you've come over," she said, breathlessly.

Ruby smiled back at her, but she felt a little uncomfortable with all this enthusiasm.

"Why?" she asked, taking off her raincoat.

Allison took it and hung it on a hook by the door. "Today is Ted's birthday," she said, "and we're having a birthday party for him at lunch time. We've invited a bunch of his friends to come over."

"That sounds like fun," said Ruby.

"Problem is that my aunt was supposed to come over and help my mom but she just phoned that she has some trouble with her car so she'll be late. Maybe she won't even make it at all. So I'm going to help. Could you help us

26

too? Mom's made a big yummy birthday cake. See. It's chocolate."

A big chocolate layer cake, decorated with jelly beans and Smarties and four yellow candles, was on the kitchen counter.

"Yum," said Ruby.

"And you could have your own loot bag. There's an extra one."

"Okay. What do we have to do?"

"We'd be in charge of the entertainment. I thought we could start the little kids off with that Spin the Bottle game to open the birthday presents. Mom was going to hire Marco Magician but remember how awful he was last year?"

Ruby nodded, remembering the grouchy man who made all the kids sit in straight rows and got so mad when they laughed at the wrong time that his red hair stuck straight out. That made them laugh even more. They laughed so hard that they fell out of their chairs and rolled on the floor.

"I'll just phone my mom to tell her that I'll be here for lunch. Okay?"

Before Ruby finished phoning, the door bell rang and the first birthday guest arrived. Ted ran to answer the door.

It was Jonathan. He was big for a four-year-old. Big and tough. His long blond hair was carefully brushed and his light blue shirt was tucked neatly into matching blue pants. He was carrying a large, brightly-wrapped present.

"Now, Jonathan," his mother said. She was a tall woman wearing pointy shoes with very high heels that made her even taller. "Remember to stay neat and tidy, because we'll be visiting Aunt Hortense after the party." She bent down and straightened his bow tie. "Give Ted his present," she said, backing out the door. "Good-bye now, dear."

"Here, Ted." Jonathan handed Ted the present. "Open it! Open it!" he said, bounding around excitedly.

Before Allison could stop him and tell him that all the presents were to be opened later, Jonathan helped Ted rip open the parcel. It was a big, scary dinosaur mask.

"It's Tyrannosaurus Rex!" said Jonathan. "Want to see how it looks?"

He put on the mask and growled so viciously at Ted that Ted scooted behind his mother and held onto her skirt.

She patted his shoulder. Then she saw Ruby.

28

"Hi Ruby," she said. "Has Allison asked you if you could give us a hand at Ted's party?"

Ruby nodded. "Sure. Sounds like fun."

"Great. I just don't know when my sister will get here."

Ruby thought Allison's mother looked quite different. She wasn't her usual tidy self, at all. Her shirt was crumpled and her eyes looked weary. Her hair was pretty messy as well. It hung down at the sides of her face instead of being pulled back into a neat pony tail as it usually was.

"It looks like it's stopped raining for now, so maybe you girls could take the boys outside to play in the backyard while I finish getting the lunch ready," she suggested, trying to tuck back a few stray wisps of hair behind her ears. "We were planning a picnic lunch outside, but the grass will still be wet after the rain, so we'd better eat around the kitchen table instead."

"We could play dinosaurs out there," suggested Ruby.

"Yeah, yeah!" shouted Jonathan. "Let's play dinosaurs!"

As he ran to follow Ruby, a wailing cry erupted from the bedroom.

"Oh dear," sighed Allison's mother. "Sounds like the baby's awake. I was hoping that she would sleep for at least another hour or so."

She rushed away to pick up the baby.

The doorbell rang again.

Allison answered it. It was Rika, a timid little girl from across the street. She wore a pretty flowered party dress. Her mother kissed her good-bye and left.

"Rika's my very best friend," Ted whispered to Ruby.

Wearing the scary Tyrannosaurus mask, Jonathan pounced at Rika, and roared his terrible dinosaur roar.

Rika squealed and hid behind Ruby's back.

Jonathan laughed and roared at her again. Louder this time.

The doorbell rang again. This time it was the twins, Jesse and Josie.

As soon as their mother had left, Jonathan roared his terrible dinosaur roar at them as well.

They roared back at him, twice as loud, since they were twins and there were two of them.

Allison's mother returned carrying the baby, Lucy, who was still howling.

Jonathan roared at her too.

The baby howled even harder.

"Allison!" shouted her mother above the roaring and the howling. "Could you and Ruby please take the kids outside until I get the baby settled again. Oh, dear. I do hope your aunt will get here soon. Maybe we should have had Marco Magician after all."

"Don't worry, Mom. Ruby and I will take the kids out and entertain them. Won't we, Rube?

Ruby nodded and made for the kitchen door.

"Come on, everyone," said Allison. "Out we go." She herded everyone out the kitchen door.

"Don't want to go outside," Rika whispered from behind Ruby.

"I'll look after you, Rika. Don't you worry now. It'll be okay. We'll have lots of fun," promised Ruby. She held Rika's small dry hand and led her out to the backyard.

Chapter 6
Entertaining Fierce Four-Year-Olds

It had stopped raining but the grass and the trees around the edge of the lawn were still wet. There was a tall board fence surrounding the whole backyard and a row of flowers along the fence. Everything looked soggy and beaten down by the rain.

As soon as they were all out in the backyard, Jonathan, still wearing the dinosaur mask, raced around, growling at the other kids.

He shouted, "I'm Tyrannosaurus Rex, king of the jungle, meat eater, and I'm coming to gobble you all up!"

The other kids squealed like frightened squirrels and scurried away across the wet grass. Jesse slipped and slid on his knees.

When Ruby helped him up, she saw wet grass stains covering his pant legs.

"We'll have to think of some game for them," said Allison.

"Remember we were going to play Spin the Bottle to open the presents?" reminded Ruby. "I'll get a pop bottle from the porch and you get the kids into a circle."

But Jonathan would not co-operate.

"Ted already opened my birthday present so I don't have to get into the circle," he told Allison.

Wearing the dinosaur mask, he frisked around the little circle, roaring his loudest dinosaur roar, while Ted spun the bottle to find out whose present to open first. The bottle pointed at Josie.

"Jesse and me got just one present because it's big enough to be from two people," she said, handing Ted a large square box.

Ted opened the box. In it was a big orange and blue beach ball.

"Don't forget to say thank you," Allison reminded him.

Before Ted could say anything, Jonathan kicked the beach ball out of his hands. Then he kicked it around the yard, shouting, "I'm Tyrannosaurus Rex, king of the Dinosaurs!"

"Just spin the bottle again, Ted," said Ruby.

The next time, the bottle pointed at Rika. Rika timidly gave Ted a small parcel tied with a red ribbon.

When Ted opened it, he found a package of

coloured gel pens in a tin.

"Cool!" he said. "All my other pens are dried out."

"Don't forget to say thank you," Allison reminded him again.

"Thanks, Rika," said Ted, grinning at her.

She smiled back shyly.

"Humph. Pens," said Jonathan. "What a boring present."

He grabbed them and tossed the whole tin into the air. The pens scattered on the wet grass.

"What a kid!" said Ruby to Allison, as they picked up the pens and put them back into the tin. "I'll keep them safe in my pocket for you, Ted. Maybe we could play Farmer in the Dell now," she suggested.

They played Farmer in the Dell twice.

"Now what? Any other ideas?" Allison asked Ruby.

"This is so-o boring!" shouted Jonathan. "You said that we were going to play Dinosaurs." He started growling and howling at the other kids again.

They all growled and howled back. Except Rika. She held Ruby's hand tightly and hid behind her like a frightened bird. Even Ted, who was usually quiet and polite, started running around and howling too.

"I know," said Ruby. "Let's play Dinosaur in the Dell."

"How do you play that?" asked Allison.

"Same as Farmer in the Dell, except it's a different kind of dinosaur in the Dell each time. Jonathan, you can be the Tyrannosaurus in the Dell, to start us off."

The new game lasted for a while, but the children soon got tired of it as well.

"This is almost as boring as Farmer in the Dell," shouted Jonathan. He growled and started to race around again.

"Can you think of any other games?" Allison asked Ruby above the roaring.

The only other game Ruby could think of was Ring around the Rosie. She did not think that these fierce four-year-olds would go for such a baby game. Even Ring around a Dinosaur likely wouldn't last long.

Out of the corner of her eye, she saw her enemy number one! Mean old Miley was stalking along the top of the back fence.

He was probably spying on them. Maybe he

was even thinking up another teasing rap about her hair. She patted her hair band to check that it was still in place.

Jonathan saw Miley and dashed over to him, growling behind the dinosaur mask. Then all the other children ran to him too.

Miley vaulted down onto the grass and cartwheeled around them.

Jonathan laughed and yelled, "Hey! Show me how to do that! I want to learn how to do a cartwheel too."

"I have an idea," Allison hissed to Ruby. "I bet Miley could help us entertain these kids. He knows lots of tricks and maybe he could even make up some neat raps for them."

"What! Ask that Mean old Miley to the party?" said Ruby. "If you do, I'm going home. Straight home.

"No, Ruby! You can't leave. Please don't leave," pleaded Allison. "You're my best friend. And you said you'd help. You promised."

Jonathan roared at Miley. Now Rika was crying behind Ruby, hiding her face in Ruby's shirt.

The other children crowded around Miley.

He swung back up onto the fence, crossed his arms, and stared down at them like a rock star up on a stage.

Dino, Dino,
Dinosaurs,
Dino, Dino,
Dinosaurs,
Roar and roar,

On up to Mars!

The fierce four-year-olds all roared up to him.

He disappeared down the other side of the fence.

"See Ruby. The kids like him. He could help us entertain them. Come on. Let's ask him. Please," pleaded Allison again.

Ruby was pretty discouraged. She and Allison were having no luck entertaining these kids.

Maybe Miley could help them. As long as he didn't start on his Fuzzy Wuzzy raps. If he did, she would go right home. No matter how much Allison pleaded.

"Well, okay," she agreed reluctantly. "I guess so."

They went out to the back lane through the gate. They saw Miley ducking behind some bushes beside the fence.

"Hey, Miley," called Allison. "We want to ask you something."

"What?" he popped up.

"We were wondering if you could come and help us entertain my little brother's friends at his birthday party," said Allison. "Please."

"You mean right now?"

Allison nodded.

Miley scowled. "Doesn't look like much fun to me," he said.

"We've got piles of food so you can have all the hot dogs and chips and lemonade you can eat when we have lunch," she said.

"Hot dogs and chips and lemonade? Is that all?" said Miley.

"And—and I bet you could have a big piece of birthday cake too," said Allison. "It's chocolate."

"Just one piece?" said Miley.

Jonathan roared at the fence. Rika was still crying behind Ruby. Louder now. And Jesse was leaning against the apple tree looking very unhappy.

"Two pieces of cake," said Ruby. "You could have two pieces. If there's not enough, I'll give you my piece. It's got real yummy chocolate icing. And Smartie decorations. I saw it."

"So what do I have to do?" he asked.

Allison said, "You could do some of those crazy acrobat tricks for the kids. And maybe tell them some of your raps. Please!"

"But no Fuzzy Wuzzy raps, though," said Ruby. "Or I'll bash you one."

Miley rubbed his nose gently. He was probably remembering when Ruby hit him on the nose with that Seraptor action figure.

"Hot dogs, chips and lemonade. And two big pieces of chocolate cake?" Miley screwed up his face while he thought about it.

"Plus a loot bag," said Ruby. "You can have my loot bag as well, I guess."

"Okay. It's a deal," said Miley.

"But no Fuzzy Wuzzy raps?" asked Ruby.

He narrowed his eyes and stared at her. "Okay. No Fuzzy Wuzzy raps," he agreed.

He held out his hand for her to slap.

Chapter 7
The Party Rap

Miley vaulted back over the fence and cart-wheeled around Jonathan.

Jonathan stopped roaring and peeked out from behind the Tyrannosaurus mask.

Miley leaped in front of him and started a rap.

'There once was a kid
Who always hid
Behind a big mask
And he wanted to ask
Oh, can I play
With you all day?
Yeah, yeah, yeah!

Jonathan laughed. "Can you show me how to do a cartwheel like that?"

"Sure. But first you have to put the mask up on the steps."

Quickly as a frisky puppy, Jonathan dashed to the back porch and put the mask up in the steps.

Miley showed him how to do a pretty good cartwheel.

Now all the other children wanted to do one as well, so Miley showed them how. Even Rika learned to do a pretty good one with Ruby's help to hold her legs out straight.

When the kids were tired, they sat on the back steps. Miley did a special birthday rap for Ted and they all joined in on the chorus.

Ted, Ted,
Got out of bed
And all he said
Would make you red.

On, on this day,
Is my birthday.
All my friends
Come over to play.

Jonathan came first
He was the worst
With a mask so big
You had to dance a jig

Then came Rika,
So sweet
She knocks you off
Offa your feet.

Then came Josie
With twin brother, Jesse
With a great big ball
And that's not all."

When the rap was over, the children clapped and yelled for him to do more.

Any minute now, Ruby was sure that Miley would start one of his Fuzzy Wuzzy raps. She knew he would not keep his promise. When he did start, she would bash his nose, then go right home, she told herself.

But he didn't say one single thing about Fuzzy Wuzzy Fuzz Balls.

Not yet, anyway.

Allison's mother called them all inside for the birthday lunch. She set an extra place for Miley beside Jonathan.

After they had gobbled up the hot dogs and chips and slurped up the lemonade, Allison's mother carried in the chocolate birthday cake with the four candles lit.

They all sang Happy Birthday to you. "Make a wish now, Ted," said his mother.

Ted shut his eyes and wished. Then he blew out all the candles on the first blow. Everyone

yelled, "Hurrah! Ted's wish will come true!"

Ruby was really glad that there was plenty of cake so she didn't have to give up her piece for Miley's second. It was as gooey and delicious as it looked.

Miley kept Jonathan and all the other kids entertained with a bunch of other rapping songs. As he was eating up his second piece, he even made up a rap for the birthday cake:

Oh, Ted's birthday cake
His mom did bake.

It's real, not a fake.
Oh, it's not a fake.
Say thanks to his mom
For great food, not dumb
And don't suck your thumb.
Just say thanks to Mom.
Say thanks to Mom.

The kids all yelled thank you to Ted's mother.

"You're welcome," she said, smiling back at them.

Ruby noticed that when she smiled, her eyes did not look as weary as before. She thought that Miley and his tricks had come along at the right time. He surely knew how to entertain a bunch of fierce four-year-olds.

After the kids had eaten until they could not stuff in one more crumb, it was time for them to go home.

They all agreed that it was the best birthday party ever. With the best entertainment. Even Jonathan agreed, although his mother was very unhappy when she came to pick him up. His clothes were a complete mess of mustard, gooey chocolate icing, and grass stains.

She pulled him out the door, saying, "I just don't know what our Aunt Hortense will think."

After all the little kids had left, it was time for Ruby and Miley to leave as well.

"Thanks, Ruby. And you too, Miley, for all your help," said Allison's mother. "I don't know what we would have done without you."

"See you next month when we get back from our granny's," said Allison. "Ted and me, we're going there on an airplane tomorrow."

"Lucky!" said Ruby. "See you when you get back."

Would Miley start teasing her, calling her Fuzzy Wuzzy on their way home, wondered Ruby. It was true that he had kept his promise so far. He had not called her Fuzzy once during the whole party. But the party was over now.

Chapter 8
A Friend Indeed

As they walked down the sidewalk, Miley seemed to be warming up to start another rap. He did a one-handed back flip and landed, splat, right in front of her.

Oh, once there was a girl
And she had a curl... he started rapping.

Then Ruby remembered her friend, Kate's magic spell. Would it work? Should she try it? Yes! She had to. It was now or never. She could not stand Miley's teasing for one more instant.

She stood as straight and tall as a pole. She clenched her fists and stared at Miley, right, smack, in the eye.

"Everybody's beautiful," she forced herself to think, as Kate had instructed. It was a really hard thought, looking at Miley's dirty, freckled face.

Then she remembered what a help he had been at Ted's party. How he had made Ted, and all the other kids laugh. Even his mother had laughed.

She concentrated. "Everybody's beautiful,"

she thought again, very, very hard.

A strange thing started to happen.

Ruby noticed that Miley's freckles looked absolutely splendid, splattered across his face! They made her think of hundreds of stars in a black sky. They were really, well, beautiful!

"Do you know that you have the most amazing freckles in this whole neighbourhood?" Ruby told him. "In fact, I bet that they're the most amazing freckles I've ever seen in my whole entire life!"

Then she smiled her biggest, most friendly smile, right straight into his face.

Miley was so astonished that he stopped rapping with his mouth still wide open. Not a sound came out.

And he stopped dancing with one foot still dangling in the air.

Then he blushed a deep crimson. He put his hand up to his red cheek.

"My—my freckles?" he stammered. "Everyone teases me about my freckles and people are always staring at me and—and..."

That was a new idea for Ruby.

"Staring at your freckles? But they are so—so interesting! I never thought freckles could be a problem. You know what? I really like them and you should be proud to own them. Not only that, you are one terrific rapper. You sure helped us out with those little kids."

Miley blushed even more. He blushed so hard that even his ears were crimson now. He tugged one red ear and scratched his red neck. He took a deep breath and stroked his nose, quite gently.

"Yeah?" he nodded. "Here's a new rap. Special for you."

That Ruby's one straight thrower
And that's no lie
Hit me on the blower
Thought I's gona die.
You know all that?
You can have him back.

He dug into his jeans pocket and pulled out Sam's Seraptor action figure. He tossed it to her.

"Thanks," laughed Ruby. "Here's the loot bag."

"No. That's okay. You can keep it. I'm stuffed to the hilt anyway."

"We could share it," she said.

Okay, okay.
What ever you say.
If you insist.
*How can I resist?"*he rapped

Ruby laughed again.

Maybe while Allison was away visiting her granny, Miley would be her summertime friend. Maybe he could even teach her a few of those neat acrobat tricks. And raps too.

Norma Charles was born in Ste. Boniface, Manitoba. She taught high school for five years, then 'retired' to be home with her four children, two boys and two girls. It was at this time that she began to write. Eventually she became a teacher/librarian in Vancouver. She has taught Creative Writing at the University of British Columbia in the Continuing Education Department, as well as doing many workshops and readings in schools and libraries. She has had eight novels for children published including *Runaway*, published by Coteau in 1999, and *Sophie Sea to Sea*, (Beach Holme) which won the British Columbia Year 2000 Book Award.

The inspiration for *Fuzzy Wuzzy*.

Galan Akin is an artist and illustrator living in Vancouver, British Columbia. Born in Oakland, California, he grew up on various islands on the west coast of Canada. He studied painting at the Nova Scotia College of Arts & Design and animation at the Emily Carr Institute of Art & Design.

If you liked this book...

you might enjoy these other Hodgepog Books:

For grades 5–8

Into the Sun
By Luanne Armstrong, illustrated by Robin LeDrew
ISBN 0-9686899-9-X $8.95

Cross My Heart
By Janet Miller, illustrated by Martin Rose

$8.95

Read these yourself in grades 3–5,
or read them to younger kids

Ben and the Carrot Predicament
by Mar'ce Merrell, illustrated by Barbara Hartmann
ISBN 1-895836-54-9 $4.95

Getting Rid of Mr. Ributus
by Alison Lohans, illustrated by Barbara Hartmann
ISBN 1-895836-53-0 $6.95

A Real Farm Girl
By Susan Ioannou, illustrated by James Rozak
ISBN 1-895836-52-2 $6.95

A Gift for Johnny Know-It-All
by Mary Woodbury, illustrated by Barbara Hartmann
ISBN 1-895836-27-1 $5.95

Mill Creek Kids
by Colleen Heffernan, illustrated by Sonja Zacharias
ISBN 1-895836-40-9 $5.95

Arly & Spike
by Luanne Armstrong, illustrated by Chao Yu
ISBN 1-895836-37-9 $4.95

A Friend for Mr. Granville
by Gillian Richardson, illustrated by Claudette Maclean
ISBN 1-895836-38-7 $5.95

Maggie & Shine
by Luanne Armstrong, illustrated by Dorothy Woodend
ISBN 1-895836-67-0 $6.95

Butterfly Gardens
by Judith Benson, illustrated by Lori McGregor McCrae
ISBN 1-895836-71-9 $5.95

The Duet
by Brenda Silsbe, illustrated by Galan Akin
ISBN 0-9686899-1-4 $5.95

Jeremy's Christmas Wish
by Glen Huser, illustrated by Martin Rose
ISBN 0-9686899-2-2 $5.95

Let's Wrestle
by Lyle Weis, illustrated by Will Milner and Nat Morris
ISBN 0-9686899-4-9 $5.95

A Pocketful of Rocks
by Deb Loughead, illustrated by Avril Woodend
ISBN 0-9686899-7-3 $5.95

Logan's Lake
by Margriet Ruurs, illustrated by Robin LeDrew
ISBN 1-9686899-8-1 $5.95

Papa's Surprises
by Constance Horne, illustrated by Mia Hansen
ISBN 0-9730831-1-5 $6.96

And for readers in grade 1-2,
or to read to pre-schoolers

Sebastian's Promise
by Gwen Molnar, illustrated by Kendra McCleskey
ISBN 1-895836-65-4 $4.95

Summer With Sebastian
by Gwen Molnar, illustrated by Kendra McClesky
ISBN 1-895836-39-5 $4.95

The Noise in Grandma's Attic
by Judith Benson, illustrated by Shane Hill
ISBN 1-895836-55-7 $4.95

Pet Fair
by Deb Loughead, illustrated by Lisa Birke
ISBN 0-9686899-3-0 $5.95